My Fox Ate My Homework

David Blaze

For Zander…

Wow! That's Awesome!

CONTENTS

FRIDAY MORNING

My teeth clicked and clacked when I stepped into my new school. Goose bumps popped up all over my arms like hot air balloons. I wasn't nervous — just cold. I knew I'd never wear shorts and a t-shirt there again.

Okay — I was a *little* nervous.

"Come on in," the sixth grade English teacher said when I stepped into her classroom. She was standing in front of a chalkboard with the name Miss Cox written across the top of it. She was older than any of the teachers I had in the city, and she had a high-pitched twang in her voice that made me shudder. "Don't be shy." She waved for me to come to her desk.

Twenty or thirty kids stared at me from their desks. My

hands felt sweaty. "Can you dance?" one of the girls shouted at me. I felt ashamed to shake my head no. I did the chicken dance once at a birthday party. I knew that didn't count.

"Class," the teacher said, wrapping an arm around my shoulders, "I'd like to introduce you to Jonah Johnson."

"Joe," I said right away. I didn't like being called Jonah. I didn't expect anyone to understand, but I didn't want to feel like a little kid.

Miss Cox chuckled. "Of course, Joe. Whatever you prefer." She motioned toward the class. "Go ahead and find a seat. We only have a few minutes left."

Some kid in a tank top jumped out of his seat and shouted, "He has to sing the song!"

I had no idea what he was talking about. My mom had begged me not to sing in public after she heard me singing in the shower one day.

Miss Cox shook her head and told the other kid to sit down. "This is Joe's first day, and he doesn't know the rules yet. I think we can give him a pass this one time." She winked at me. "Anyone who's late has to sing a song in front of the class. We'll teach it to you later, Joe. Besides, I'm sure you have a good reason for being late on your first day."

I had a really good reason. It was Friday and I didn't want to be there at all! Why couldn't my mom let me start this school on a Monday like everyone else? She had to pry me out of my bedroom kicking and screaming. She even threatened to dress me like the little girl she always wanted.

2

I walked through the rows of desks to the back of the room. I didn't want to sit near the front because that's where you get asked all the questions.

"Not here," some big kid with wavy blond hair growled at me before I could sit at the only open seat. He was so big he looked like he was supposed to be in the ninth grade. He stared at the desk when he spoke. "That seat is reserved."

The desk had dust on it, so I knew no one had sat there in a long time. "I'll find another seat next week. Let me sit here for now."

"Maybe I didn't make myself clear, Jonah," he hissed. "This seat is reserved, Jonah."

My face felt hot when he called me that name twice. "It's Joe," I reminded him. "Call me Joe."

He stood straight up, kicked his chair back, and waved a fist at me. I gulped. He was the tallest sixth grader I'd ever seen. He was wearing a gray t-shirt and gray shorts.

Miss Cox appeared by my side out of nowhere. "Do we have a problem here, Shane?"

The kid snickered, shook his head, and sat back down.

Miss Cox took a deep breath and motioned for me to follow her. She led me right back to the front row of desks and an open seat. I had been there for less than five minutes, and I was already embarrassed out of my mind. It was going to be a long day.

"Don't forget about the paper due on Monday morning," Miss Cox said to the room. "I want to see three paragraphs about your best friend. I'll be grading for grammar, punctuation, and speech."

I raised my hand. "Speech?"

Miss Cox smiled. "Yes, Joe. In this class we work on presentation skills. Anything you write, you say in front of the class." She lowered her voice. "I know it's short notice, but is this something you can do by Monday? I heard you're a writer."

I didn't have any problem with writing three paragraphs. I was a writer for my other school's newsletter. But making a speech in front of the class? I gulped. I'd never done that before. I looked up at Miss Cox and said the only thing I could say to save myself from more embarrassment. "Sure, no problem."

The class bell rang, and everyone jumped out of their seats. There was so much noise and talking in the room I couldn't concentrate on how scared I was about Monday morning. I knew I shouldn't have started this school on a Friday. I mean, who starts school on a Friday?

"Are you okay?" the girl next to me asked. She had two ponytails and big dimples.

I stood up and slung my backpack over my shoulder. "I don't know yet."

She chuckled and stood next to me with a huge smile. "My name's Melissa."

I pulled my new class schedule out of my backpack. "Do you know where Room 104 is?"

She snatched the paper out of my hand and headed toward the door. "Yeah. That's my next class too. Follow me."

At least there was one friendly person at the school.

She had a bit of a twang in her voice, but not as bad as Miss Cox. I'd have to get used to it in the country.

"Where are you from?" Melissa asked when we walked into the hall.

"Orlando," I said proudly. She had to be impressed with a city boy like me coming to this small country town in Alabama. She smiled and kept walking.

I felt obligated to ask her some questions back. I wasn't a big talker, but I knew most kids liked talking about themselves. Melissa was the only person willing to be my friend so far. I couldn't risk losing that. "Where are *you* from?"

She stopped in front of Room 104, looked directly into my eyes, and said, "I came from my mama." She burst out laughing.

She didn't stop laughing, and it was so contagious I couldn't help but laugh with her.

The laughing stopped when Shane appeared by my side. I'm not short, but he was at least four inches taller than me. He was trouble — I couldn't show him any fear.

"We need to talk," Shane blurted out. He didn't look angry like before. I didn't know how much I could trust him, and I didn't know how much time there was until the next class started. "It'll only take a minute," he pleaded.

I glanced at Melissa. She shrugged her shoulders and walked into the classroom. "I'll save you a seat," she promised.

I looked back up at Shane. "It's fun to mess with the new kid. I don't want any trouble."

Shane frowned like he was hurt. "I'm sorry about earlier," he confessed.

I wasn't sure how to respond. All I could say was, "Oh. Okay."

He smiled for the first time and punched my shoulder playfully. "So you're a writer?"

This was going a lot better than I expected. It wouldn't be hard making friends after all. "I dabble here and there," I proclaimed. "I won an award at my other school."

Shane's eyes got big. "That's awesome!" he shouted.

Another kid wearing a tank top joined us. His hair was cut like a sailor's. It took me a second to realize he was the kid from Miss Cox's class who had tried to make me sing a song.

"Hey, Joe," Shane said to me. "This is my best friend, Sam." They pounded fists. "Isn't it funny that Miss Cox wants us to write a paper about our best friends?"

My stomach churned. I had a bad feeling this wasn't going so well after all.

"Sam and I grew up together," Shane continued. "We like to go fishing and hunting."

I tried to step backwards toward the classroom. I already knew what he was going to ask me.

"Say," Shane said to me, "you're a writer and we're friends now, right?" He followed every step I took. I was pretty sure we weren't friends.

He reached out and grabbed my shirt collar with one hand. "Where are you going?" He tightened his grip. "I'm gonna need you to write my paper for me, Jonah."

I love to write, but not under threats and not for someone else. "My name is Joe."

Shane and Sam both snickered as he released my shirt and straightened it out. "This is going to be a long year for you if you don't write it. And you'll be very, very sorry." He shoved me into the room. I stumbled and fell flat on my back. Shane towered over me, smirked, and said, "Make the right decision."

The two bullies high fived each other and disappeared down the hall. I stared up at the ceiling and wished I was invisible.

"Are you okay?" Melissa asked after I got up and sat next to her. "Shane is a big bully. If you give him what he wants then he'll never leave you alone."

She was right. But to be honest — I was scared to death of the big kid! I didn't know yet my whole world would be turned upside down after school that day, but I knew right then and there what choice I would make about writing Shane's paper.

FRIDAY AFTERNOON

I went straight to my room when I got home and lay on the bed. It was so lumpy that my back had hurt all morning after tossing and turning in it all night. It's weird to call it my room and my bed when just yesterday I was living somewhere else.

My mom knocked on my door. "Is it safe to come in here?"

This was my great-grandma's house, and it had been built in 1930. The floors creaked and the walls smelled like smoke. I wasn't sure any room in this house was safe. "It's open," I told her.

She sat on the edge of the bed. "It's hard leaving everything behind. But I have to do what's best for us." She glanced around the room. "Right now this is it."

I sat up and stared at the dirty white wall in front of me. "I know." She had lost her job, and we had nowhere else to go. Great-grandma had left this place to my mom in her will. "Thank you, Mom." She was a warrior and she'd never give up.

She leaned against my shoulder. "Now you're talking to me?" We both laughed. "How was your first day of school, Mister?"

All I could think about was Shane's order to write his paper. It made me feel sick. How could I write three paragraphs for him anyways? He had only told me that he and the other guy liked to hunt and fish. I definitely did not want to write it. On the other hand, I definitely did not want to get beat up.

"It was okay," I told my mom. "I get to do some writing — like I did for the other school." I thought about telling her the truth, but she already had too many things to worry about.

She hugged my shoulders. "That's great, Jonah! You're a wonderful writer." She was the only one allowed to call me Jonah.

We both jumped when a knock at the front door echoed through the walls. My mom stood up and asked me, "Who could that be?"

"Maybe it's the pizza delivery man," I said with high hopes.

She shook her head and walked out of the room. I followed her to make sure everything was okay. My mom had spent a lot of summers in this town many years ago, but she didn't know anyone there now — except for my uncle.

She opened the door. "Hello," said a big, chubby man in a striped suit. He smiled wide and waved a smelly cigar. "Miss Johnson?"

"Yes?" she replied. "Can I help you?"

"I'm sorry to disturb you on such a beautiful day." He bowed slightly to reveal an almost bald head. "My name is Mitch Connors, and I'm from the IRS." He cleared his throat. "My condolences for the loss of your grandmother." He sounded sincere.

"Thank you," she said. She pulled me forward. "This is my son, Jonah."

Mr. Connors extended his hand to me. As I shook it, I said, "Please call me Joe." He nodded.

The man returned his attention to my mom. "Miss Johnson, we need to discuss your late grandmother's property taxes. She never paid them."

I had no idea what he was talking about, but my mom didn't have any money. Mr. Connors seemed like a nice man, but I didn't want him to be there anymore.

"Jonah," my mom said, "go out back and make sure the chicken coop is locked before it gets dark." I wish I could say I didn't know what she was talking about, but I had spent enough time there to know my great-grandma kept a bunch of chickens out back.

I didn't want to leave my mom stranded there with that man. I was scared he was going to give her more bad news. She looked at me and winked.

"Go on now," my mom said. "Everything's going to be okay." I wanted to believe her, but I knew it wasn't true.

"It was nice to meet you, young man," Mr. Connors said as I walked away. I didn't respond to him. I shook my head and marched straight to the back of the house.

I could still hear him talking before I slammed the door. "This house will belong to us on Tuesday unless you can pay the $14,112.00 that's due."

I already knew we'd be living somewhere else next week. That was a good thing because I wasn't a big fan of the mosquitoes out there. And now I didn't have to worry about Shane or the paper about my best friend. Which was another good thing. I didn't have a best friend.

I stood in front of a wooden shack outside the back door. It had a half moon carved into it. This wasn't the chicken coop — no sir. This was the outhouse.

My mom used to tell me how houses didn't have indoor plumbing in the old days. The toilets were outside in these outhouses. This house was upgraded years ago and there was a toilet inside now, but this magnificent building was still there.

I passed the outhouse and headed for the chicken coop. A large area of land around it was fenced in so the chickens could come out to eat and get some exercise. The chicken coop reminded me of the tree house I had in the city (except it was on the ground). It was made out of wood and had a door so a person could walk into it. The chickens laid their eggs in there.

They were already in the coop. There were only twelve chickens left. Great-grandma used to have a lot more, but she always said one disappeared every now and then — like a magic trick.

Right there in the back was Old Nelly. She was my great-grandma's favorite chicken. As my great-grandma got older, she swore Old Nelly talked to her and laid golden eggs.

Now, let's get one thing straight — Old Nelly didn't lay golden eggs. None of that chicken's eggs could be sold and they were not safe for human consumption. Old Nelly only laid rotten eggs!

I froze when I stepped out of the coop — half in fear, half in amazement.

An animal I had never seen before stared at me. It looked a lot like a dog, but it had to be something else. It wasn't very big — the size of a Scottish terrier like our neighbor in Orlando had. It was a bright brown color — almost orange. The end of its tail was white, just like its chest. All four paws were black.

There were two things about this animal I would never forget. It had the bluest eyes I had ever seen, like the ocean. And it was smiling at me.

I bent down slowly and picked up a stick. I wasn't afraid of the animal. I had always wanted my own dog and this was my chance. I tossed the stick to the side and shouted, "Fetch!"

The animal jumped like it was going to run away. Then it looked over at the stick and back at me. I don't want to sound like a crazy person, but I'm telling you this creature shook its head no at me.

"What are you?" I whispered. "You're not a dog. If you were then you'd have a collar." I took a step toward the animal with my hands out to show I wasn't a threat. Something told me this creature could be my friend. "This is nuts. You've got to be some kind of dog. Where's your collar?"

I stopped a few feet in front of the animal I hoped was a dog. It stared at me with its blue eyes, and then looked around like it wanted to make sure no one else was watching. It stood up slowly on its two hind legs — just like a human! What it did next took my breath away.

"I don't know," the animal said like a child. "Where's *your* collar?"

I fell flat on my butt and scooted backwards with

my hands. My great-grandma had said Old Nelly talked to her. Now that dog-like animal was talking to me. Maybe that land made people crazy.

"Jonah!" my mom screamed from the back door. "Where are you? You better not be in the outhouse!"

I couldn't move anymore when the animal walked up to me like a human. "I'm a fox," he said. "Don't tell anyone you saw me here." It winked at me and raced toward the fence. I stood up and watched in disbelief as it jumped over the fence and ran out of the yard.

LATER THAT AFTERNOON

"You locked the chicken coop, right?" my mom asked when I walked back into the house. I couldn't remember, but that didn't matter at the moment — so I nodded.

"We're going to stay with Uncle Mike for a while," she said.

I could barely understand what she was saying. All I could think about was the talking fox. It was the most amazing thing I'd ever seen, but I couldn't tell anyone about him — not even my mom.

"We have to be out of here by Tuesday morning," she continued. "So we'll make the best of it for the weekend."

I sat at the dining room table and tried to process what she said. Uncle Mike grew up in this town and never left. I'd still have to go to the same school and face Shane. But more importantly, we had to stay here in case the fox came back. "We can't leave," I begged.

My mom sat next to me. "What are you talking about? You don't even like it here." All I could do was look at her and plead with my eyes. "Don't give me that look, Mister. I already feel bad enough as it is."

I put a hand on her shoulder. "It's not your fault," I

assured her.

She wiped her nose. "So I was thinking we could go to the farmers market tomorrow morning and sell some eggs. It'll be fun. I used to do it in the summers every Saturday with my grandma." She paused and smiled at me. "This is our only chance to do it together."

There was a sparkle in her eyes. She looked excited about it, and I couldn't disappoint her. "Sure, Mom. We can do that."

She stood up and wrapped her arms around me. "It's a shame, really." She looked out the kitchen window and into the yard. "I had some of the best times of my life here."

I wondered if she had ever seen any talking animals there. I wanted to tell her about the fox so bad, but I couldn't for two reasons. One was the fox told me not to. He didn't threaten me — he was trying to protect himself. The other was I didn't want my mom to think I was losing my mind.

"Did you have any homework?" she asked.

My stomach churned when I thought about the paper due in Miss Cox's class. I consider myself a writer, but I didn't have a best friend to write about. It would have to be about my mom — not a smart move for a new kid like me. Shane and Sam would tease me all year about it. I couldn't believe he had told me to write his paper!

"I have to write something for my English class," I told her. It wasn't a lie, and it kept me from having to explain everything that had happened in school.

"Okay," she said. "You should go ahead and do that.

We may not have a lot of free time this weekend."

I agreed with her and stood up to head for my room.

"Just a second, Mister," my mom commanded. "What would you like for dinner?"

I didn't have an appetite. My head was swirling with so many thoughts that it began to hurt. "I'm going to lie down for a while. I'm not hungry."

She nodded her head. "Come get me if you need anything."

I jumped into my bed as soon as I closed my bedroom door. The mattress was so lumpy that I was sure there were bricks inside of it. It wasn't uncomfortable to lie on, but after eight hours of sleep it always left my back in pain. There was no reason to complain about it — we were only going to be there for a few more days.

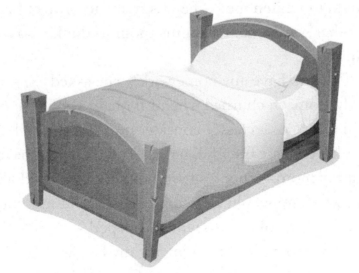

I was exhausted and needed a power nap before I wrote anything. Every time my eyes shut I could see the fox's blue eyes staring back at me. I wondered if I'd ever see him again.

FRIDAY NIGHT

I jumped out of my sleep when I heard a ruckus outside. The room was dark so I knew the sun had gone down. I looked at my watch and saw it was midnight!

I only felt half awake, and my back was killing me. I wished I could sleep on the floor, but that place had roaches that came out at night. I had heard them crunch under my feet when I got up to use the bathroom the night before. They disappeared the moment I turned the lights on.

I jumped again when a door banged shut from outside. *The chicken coop!* I suddenly realized I did forget to lock it.

I hopped out of the bed and shuddered every time I felt a crunch under my shoes. I walked down the hall and into the kitchen. My mom was nowhere to be found, and I didn't expect her to be — she was sound asleep. I grabbed a flashlight off the kitchen counter and walked out the backdoor and into the yard.

The outhouse looked scary in the dark — like a haunted house. The moon that night was shaped like a trimmed fingernail and not giving off much light. I flicked the flashlight on and marched toward the chicken coop. I had to lock it before the chickens got out and put themselves in danger.

I dropped the flashlight when it focused on two blue eyes. The fox was walking out of the chicken coop. I was happy to see him again, but what was he doing in there?

"You don't want to go in there for ten to fifteen minutes," the fox said. "And you might want to light a candle." He waved a paw in front of his nose like something stank.

And it did.

The putrid odor made me feel sick. The fox was covered in something wet and slimy. I knew exactly what it was.

"Old Nelly," I whispered.

The fox shook its body rapidly from side to side so the rotten egg yolk flew off of him in every direction. "That crazy old chicken threw her eggs at me! She attacked me for no reason."

I suspected Old Nelly had her reasons. She had never thrown her eggs at me. "Maybe she got nervous," I explained. "You shouldn't be in there at night."

The fox smiled and said, "I like you, Jonah. I think we're gonna be good friends."

I couldn't help but smile back. It didn't feel weird talking to the fox, and he was nice. "Wait a second," I said. "How did you know my name? And please call me Joe."

The fox turned and walked toward the fence area he had jumped over earlier that day. "The other human with you yelled your name earlier. She said something about the outhouse."

That made sense. "Where are you going?" I asked. "I have so many things I want to ask you."

The fox stopped walking and faced me. "I need to get some dinner." He looked back at the chicken coop. "I missed my last meal." He shook his head like he was disappointed. "And there's a river down the road. I need to wash up."

I had to agree with him on the last part. "That's a good idea. You smell like wet farts."

He huffed, crouched on all four paws, and raced out of the yard.

I locked the chicken coop and went back into the house. I felt a lot better after talking with the fox. I wondered how old he was. Probably the same age as me (eleven) — maybe a year or two younger. And I wondered once again when I would see him next. He liked the chicken coop. I'd try to meet him there again tomorrow.

I turned the kitchen and living room lights on — not a roach in sight. I was wide awake now, and it was the perfect time to write my paper for school. I grabbed two sheets out of my backpack and a number 2 pencil. That was funny. *Number 2.* Made me think of the outhouse.

I titled the first page *My Best Friend.* There were only three paragraphs to go. I couldn't think of anything. Why was this so hard? I loved to write and could probably write a book. I could warm up by writing Shane's paper. I knew who his best friend was, and I could make everything else up.

No. That was a horrible idea. I crumpled the second piece of paper and threw it in the trash. I didn't want to entertain the idea of writing Shane's paper for him. But still, my life would be easier at school if I did it. And I wouldn't have to walk the halls scared for my life.

I gave up for the night and pulled out a magazine for boys. It had articles about nature and science. Maybe I'd write for that magazine one day.

I fell out of my seat when something rapped on the kitchen window. My heart felt like it was going to explode. It thumped on my chest like it was trying to escape. I tried to ignore the noise in the kitchen, hoping it was only my imagination — but it happened again.

There's no reason to be afraid. I took a few steps toward the kitchen and peered around the corner at the window. I didn't see anything. It had to be nothing more than a branch scraping against the window. It was windy outside.

I nearly fainted when a small face pressed against the window. Once I caught my breath, I realized it was the fox. He laughed, stuck his tongue out at me, and pointed a paw toward the front door.

Was he asking to come in? He disappeared from the window as quickly as he had appeared. I scratched my head and walked to the front door.

I had misunderstood him. Why would a fox want to come inside?

I opened the door to find the fox standing there, smiling. "Did you miss me?" he asked. He walked right past me and into the house. "I've never been inside a human's den."

I sighed and closed the door. It was pretty awesome to have him there. Thankfully he didn't smell like wet farts any more. He was used to being outside, and I had to lay down some rules. "Just make sure you don't pee on the carpet," I warned him.

He jumped on the couch and sat up in the corner. "I won't if you won't."

I laughed and sat on the couch with him. "It's a shame I won't be here much longer. You're the coolest animal I've ever met."

He narrowed his eyes. "What do you mean?"

"We can't stay here," I confided in him. "We don't have enough money. We're leaving in a few days to stay with my uncle Mike." Why was I telling him this?

The fox looked confused. "I don't know what that means, but in my neck of the woods, if you don't have enough of something then you work as hard as you have to until you do."

He was a fox, so I didn't expect him to understand. "I'm a kid," I told him. "I don't have a way to make money."

He huffed and pointed with one of his black paws to the magazine I was reading earlier. It was upside down on the floor. "What about that?"

I threw my hands up. "What about it?"

The fox jumped off the couch, grabbed the magazine, and handed it to me. "Those kids look like they're getting enough of what they want."

What kids was he talking about? I studied the back of the magazine. I saw exactly what he meant, and I knew he was right. The kids in the picture had fistfuls of dollars and were surrounded by toys. They got all of that by selling candy the company in the advertisement gave them.

"My mom won't let me do it," I told him. I wanted to sell the candy before, but my mom said no. She didn't want me going door to door and meeting strangers. She said it wasn't safe. I tried to argue with her, but she was right. Meeting new people was too scary.

"The other human?" the fox asked. I nodded. "If this could help you get enough of what you need, then I don't understand why it's a problem."

He was making too much sense. I couldn't make enough money selling candy to pay for the house, but I could make enough to help get it back for my mom.

I went to the laptop computer my mom had set up in the corner of the room. It was already connected to the internet. I typed in the web address on the back of the magazine.

The web site was filled with pictures of money and prizes. I felt excited and confident about this. If those kids on the website could make a lot of money — then so could I!

I whipped my wallet out of my back pocket when the website asked for a credit card. I don't have my own credit card, but my mom had given me one of hers for emergencies only. This was definitely an emergency!

"I'm gonna do it," I turned and told the fox. "I'm gonna get a box of candy and make a lot of money to help my mom."

"Sounds like a good idea," he said. "But if one box can get you all of that (he was pointing to the money and prizes on the screen), then imagine what you could do with two boxes."

I agreed with him and changed the quantity to two. We needed the money as soon as possible, so I opted to pay extra for overnight shipping. "I'm glad you're here, fox," I admitted to him. "I think we'll be good friends."

His blue eyes glowed brighter and his tail wagged. "It's time for me to go home, Joe." He walked to the front door on his two hind legs and waited for me to open it.

"Will I see you again?" I asked as I opened the door and let him out.

He rubbed his chin. "It depends."

"It depends on what?" I wondered aloud.

He took a step back. "It depends on if you take a bath or not. You're the one who smells like wet farts now."

I smelled my armpits. I didn't smell anything. I wanted

to ask him what he was talking about, but he ran off laughing. "Made you smell your armpits!"

SATURDAY MORNING

I made coffee and bacon for my mom before she woke up. She could barely walk or talk until she had her coffee. And as far as the bacon — that was for me.

We collected all of the eggs that day to take to the farmers market.

"Thank you for locking the chicken coop last night," she said before we got there. "Have to protect them from wild animals."

I nearly choked on a laugh. I couldn't imagine the fox as a wild animal.

"This is our table," my mom said after we got into the park at the farmers market. She pointed to one in the middle of dozens of others. Some of the other tables were covered with fruits and vegetables. One had a massage chair next to it with a sign that said it cost five dollars for five minutes. My first thought was, *This is where all the health nuts shop.*

People were everywhere — wearing jeans and

overalls, walking from table to table and talking to each other like they were having the best time of their lives. That place was as crowded as the theme parks in Orlando.

Someone blasted country music from a speaker overhead. I could smell hamburgers being grilled from a booth further down the park. This place was awesome!

"Put those right there," my mom said. She was pointing to the middle of our table. I knew she was talking about the eggs we had hauled there. Our arms were full with cartons that were cut in half.

"Good morning, ya'll," said an old guy wearing a straw hat and staring at the eggs. He had a strong country accent. "Glad ya'll could join us. My name is Jim Bob."

My mom wiped her hands on her pants. "Hi, Jim Bob. We're happy to be here. My name is Julie, and this is my son Jonah."

"Call me Joe," I told him right away.

He gave me a weird look, shook his head, laughed, and pointed to the eggs. "How much?"

"It's six dollars for half a dozen eggs," my mom said proudly.

Mr. Bob whistled. "That's too rich for my blood. I can get a whole dozen at the grocery store for half that price."

My mom crossed her arms. "You're right, Jim

Bob. But the chickens that laid the eggs you get at the grocery store were raised on an overcrowded ranch. They were stressed out all the time. They may have ingested pesticides and ate each other's poop."

Mr. Bob scrunched his face in disgust. I did too.

"Now *my* chickens were raised on a small farm by my grandma," my mom continued. "She hand fed them every day and talked to them like they were her own children." She put a hand on my back. "Those chickens were loved. They're happy. Happy chickens make better tasting eggs."

Jim Bob walked away with two dozen eggs!

"That was amazing, Mom!" I looked at her with

nothing but respect. I hoped I could be like her one day. "You've gotta teach me how to do that."

She took a deep breath and laughed. "Don't get used to it. They really are overpriced." She leaned against the table. "Your great-grandma never came here to make money. She just wanted to interact with people."

I didn't know a lot about my great-grandma, but she seemed pretty cool. I couldn't help but wonder how she survived all these years by selling eggs. She never had a job, and my great-grandfather passed away long before I was born.

"How did she do it?" I asked my mom.

"How did she do what?"

"How did she live without any money?" I wondered aloud. She left this world without a penny to her name.

My mom shrugged her shoulders. "I'm sure she had government assistance. And your great-grandfather Ray made sure she was taken care of before he passed away."

An elderly couple stepped up to our table and smiled. "What do we have here?" the woman asked. Her hair was gray in the front and the rest of it was brown. The man with her was bald with a long gray mustache and bushy gray eyebrows.

"Don't be silly," the old man told the woman. "I'd know these eggs anywhere." He stared at me and squinted an eye. "These are Rita's eggs. What are you doing with them?"

I had no idea who Rita was or why this guy thought the eggs were hers. He was a lunatic, and I didn't want to deal with it. He scared me. "Mom?" I said, looking up at her and swallowing hard.

My mom laughed. "My name is Julie, and this is my son, Jonah," she said to the couple. She patted me on the back. "Rita was my grandma."

"Call me Joe," I whispered.

"Oh, dear child," the old woman said in a

comforting voice. "I'm so happy to meet you. Your grandma was a wonderful person." She stared at the table for a minute like she was lost in memories. "My name is Martha Hunter." She pointed to the man. "This is my husband, Jonathan Hunter."

My mom stepped around the table and shook the couples' hands. "Did you know her well?" she asked Mrs. Hunter.

Mr. Hunter cleared his throat. "Are you kidding me?" he laughed. "The two of them never stopped talking!" He looked at me and winked. "I had to get a new bottle of Aspirin every week."

"Don't listen to him," his wife said. "He's old and bitter." She shook her head and grabbed my mom's hands. "I miss her dearly. We must get together and talk sometime."

My mom smiled. "Thank you."

Mr. Hunter grabbed his wife's hand and pulled on it. "Let's keep moving, Martha. The sun is hotter than a bonfire right now." He wiped his forehead. "Let these young people work on their tans."

I half waved at Mr. Hunter as they walked away. He was scary at first but overall a really cool guy.

My mom patted her pants leg. That meant her cell phone was vibrating. She answered the call and held up a finger to me, signaling she needed a minute.

Her conversation went like this: "Uh huh. Uh

huh. Yeah. Uh huh. Okay."

She put a palm over the receiver and looked at me. "It's Uncle Mike. Something about a job." She took her palm away from the receiver and spoke into it again. "Yeah, I'm still here. Just a minute."

I loved listening to these kinds of conversations where I could only hear one person. *Not.* It was like trying to put a puzzle together, and all the pieces were the wrong sizes.

"This is going to take a few minutes," my mom said to me. "I need to step away. Can you handle the table?"

I looked around at all the people at the farmers market. There had to be hundreds of them. None of them were coming to our table. "Yeah — I think I'll be okay."

She stepped through the crowd to the other side of the park where there were empty benches. I hoped it was good news for my mom. She loved to work and be around people.

"Hello, Orlando," some girl said to me. I looked across the table and saw my only friend at school. I thought her name was Melissa. Yeah, that was it. She was the one with big dimples. She gave me a wide grin.

"Hey," I said. "What are you doing here?" I was happy to see her, but tried not to show too much excitement.

"I like to get crazy on the weekends," she said, bobbing her head to the slow country music playing overhead.

I laughed because I knew she was kidding. At least I hoped she was kidding. She frowned like she was hurt, then burst out laughing. "Got ya!"

"I'm glad you're here," I told her with a smile.

She smiled back. "Are you selling a lot of eggs?"

I was too embarrassed to tell her we had only

sold eggs to one person. "We're doing okay," I lied.

She shook her head. "No, you're not." I shrugged my shoulders like I was confused by what she had said. "Everyone who comes here on a regular basis knows these are Rita's eggs."

"What's that supposed to mean?" I asked with my arms crossed. I didn't know my great-grandma very well, but the people around here better not have said anything bad about her.

Melissa picked up a half carton of eggs and studied them. "Rita always had rotten eggs in her cartons."

"She thought they were golden eggs," I whispered.

Melissa put the carton down. "So, did you start on your paper, Mr. Writer?"

I shook my head. "Not yet. I'm working on something big."

"Can't wait," she said and clicked her tongue. "Do yourself a favor and stay away from Shane. He doesn't do any of his own work." She turned to walk away. "Someone has to stand up to him."

I had to agree with her. I just wasn't sure if I was the right person to do it. I had never been in a fight, and I wanted to keep it that way.

My mom came back to the table with a smile on her face. "Okay, so... Uncle Mike's job had a position open up, and they want to see me right away."

"Today?" I asked, holding up my hands.

She sighed. "I hope that's not a problem."

It wasn't a problem at all. I had another chance to talk to the fox, and I didn't want to pass that up — but there was one thing I had to do before we left.

"Those hamburgers smell good," I said, holding my stomach as it growled. I don't know how long we were there, but I had smelled the hamburgers grilling the entire time with spices like garlic and pepper.

"I could use one too, but I'm not sure we made enough money for that…" my mom said, picking up the egg cartons.

I was so desperate for a hamburger that I pleaded with her. "We made twenty-four dollars. How can it not be enough for two hamburgers?"

My mom smirked and spoke in a very serious voice. "People around here are crazy. They charge six dollars for half a dozen eggs." She shook her head like it was an unfair price. "If they charge for hamburgers the same way…" She started to laugh and couldn't finish the sentence. So she tried again. "If they charge for hamburgers the same way, then it'll be six dollars for half a hamburger." She snorted and laughed like she had just told the funniest joke in the world.

All I could do was shake my head. Maybe we had been in the sun too long.

SATURDAY AFTERNOON

As soon as we got home, I opened the back door to see if I could find the fox. He was nowhere to be found. Maybe he was by the chicken coop again. "I'm gonna check on the chickens," I told my mom.

"Not right now," she said, buttoning up a fancy dress shirt. "Close the door and come here." I sighed and closed the door slowly, hoping to catch a glimpse of the fox.

Nothing. Nada.

"Listen to me carefully," my mom said when I joined her in the living room. "I need to go take some tests for this job. I may be gone for a few hours."

I didn't have any problem with that. It would give me more time to find the fox. It could also be my only chance to use the outhouse.

"Do not leave this house for any reason," my mom stressed. "I want you to stay right here and write your paper for school if you haven't done it yet." She nodded her head slowly like she wanted me to nod with her to show I understood.

"Okay," I murmured. It wasn't fair, and I couldn't tell her why, but I did need to write the three paragraphs about my best friend. This would be the perfect time to do it.

She put on some lipstick and headed for the front door. "Call me if you need anything. Don't forget there's a pizza in the fridge." She hesitated after she opened the front door. I thought for sure she wasn't going to leave.

"Love you, Mom," I encouraged her. "See you when you get back."

She smiled and said she loved me too before closing the door. I waited until I heard the car pull away before I rushed out the back door. The chickens were roaming their fenced area. The coop was empty. I searched the entire yard. My heart sank when I knew for sure the fox wasn't there.

I went back inside and grabbed another two sheets of paper from my backpack. I sat on the couch and placed the paper on the coffee table in front of it. I didn't know what had happened to the one from the night before, so I started over again with *My Best Friend* written across the top of one sheet.

I couldn't go any further. I wasn't sure if I even had a best friend.

A large car or truck skidded in the driveway in front of the house. A loud horn honked. I didn't move because I had no idea who it was. My heart stopped when someone banged on the front door. I tried not to move, hoping whoever it was didn't realize I was there.

They banged on the door again. I shook every time their fist hit the door. "Delivery for Jonah Johnson!" a man's voice shouted from outside.

Me? I had a delivery?

Oh yeah! The candy!

I jumped up and raced for the door. I was scared I was too late when I heard the delivery truck start back up. I threw the door open and yelled, "Wait!"

A big man wearing shorts jumped out of the truck. "Jonah Johnson?" I nodded my head. "Almost missed you, buddy."

He walked over to me with a large box in his hands and a tablet shaped like a clipboard. He set the box on the ground by me. "Sign here." He was pointing to a spot on the tablet as he handed a pen to me.

I signed it, thanked him, grabbed my box of candy and went back inside. I couldn't wipe the smile off my face because I was so excited about all the money I was about to make. I ripped the box open and pulled out two smaller boxes full of chocolate candy bars.

I'd have to write my paper later because it was time to get down to business. I stepped out of the house with the boxes in both hands and closed the door. I didn't have a key so I couldn't lock the door. I doubted it would be a problem since we lived in the country and there were only a handful of houses on this road.

My mom said I couldn't leave the house, but I had to do it for both of us. She was going back to work to make some money, and now I had the chance to make some money too. She'd have to be proud of me for helping out. Together, we could get this house back.

I walked out of the yard with my candy and headed down the dirt road. There were two more houses on the right side and three on the left. I'd stop at each one and sell as much candy as possible. If it went well, and I sold all the candy, I'd do this every Saturday.

No one was home at the first house. I was disappointed, but I refused to give up this early.

Maybe they went to the farmers market. I could check back later.

No one was home at the second house either. Now I was getting worried. There were only three more houses on this street. I wasn't willing to go down any other streets because I didn't want to get lost.

A young man opened the door at the third house. He was wearing a motorcycle jacket and had earrings in both ears. There was a cigarette in his left hand. "Yeah?" he said.

I gulped. I couldn't say anything. I had pictured this moment perfectly in my head. I was supposed to introduce myself and be friendly. That didn't happen.

"Are you okay, kid?" the guy asked.

I cleared my throat and held up one of the boxes. I could only say one word, and it was in a squeaky voice I didn't recognize as my own. "Candy?"

The man sighed. "Ah, man. I bought a box of chocolate the other day from another kid."

Strike three. This was the third house, and I still hadn't sold any candy. I lowered the box and turned to walk away. I felt embarrassed for some reason.

"Hold on, kid," the man said. He threw his cigarette down and stomped on it before blowing a puff of smoke out his mouth. "How much?"

I faced him and cleared my throat again. "A dollar a bar."

He huffed. "Give me five of them." His voice was raspy like he didn't want to do it. He reached for his wallet and pulled out a five dollar bill.

I handed him the five chocolate bars and accepted his money. "Thank you!"

He just said, "Yeah," and slammed his door.

Okay. Now I was getting somewhere. There were two more houses to go. Thank goodness I didn't give up earlier. Things were looking up!

No one was home at the fourth house. I rubbed my forehead and panicked. The two boxes had twenty bars of chocolate each. Forty bars in all!

What was I thinking? I had thirty-five bars left and there was no way I could sell them all at one house.

I still had to sell as many as I could. My mom would be home soon and I'd have to explain all of this to her. I did not want to do that. I couldn't give up.

I knocked on the sixth door. No one answered. It was over. It was *all* over. I was going to be in so much trouble.

"Hello," said an old man's voice before I turned away. "I don't believe it. You're the kid who stole Rita's eggs." He waited a second, laughed, and then turned to someone behind him. "Martha, come here. It's Rita's great-grandson."

Mrs. Hunter was by his side within seconds. She smiled. "Oh, dear child. Come in, come in." I wasn't supposed to go into strangers' homes, but I had met these people with my mom just a couple of hours earlier. Not that it mattered — I had to get home before my mom did.

"I can't stay," I told them.

Mr. Hunter narrowed his eyes. "What brings you here, Joe?"

I was surprised he remembered my name and said it right. "I'm selling some candy and wanted to see if you wanted any."

Mr. Hunter shook his head. "I love chocolate, but my doctor won't let me touch it."

And there it was. Did you hear it? It was the sound of my complete failure. I did everything I could to keep from crying. "Thanks anyways," I told them. My mom was going to kill me.

"Wait a second, child," Mrs. Hunter said. "Why are you selling the chocolate?"

I hesitated. "I want to help my mom."

Mrs. Hunter made a sound from her throat that sounded like *awwwww*. "You're a good boy." She turned to her husband. "It's up to you," she said to him. "Rita was my best friend." She walked away and left Mr. Hunter in the doorway facing me.

"Come to think of it," Mr. Hunter said, "I never

liked my doctor much." He pointed to the boxes in my hands. "How much is the chocolate?"

"One dollar each," I told him. He was only going to buy one — so it didn't matter. I wished he'd hurry up, though. My mom could already be home. She'd call the cops because the door was unlocked and I wasn't there.

"How many do you have left?" he asked. He needed to stop wasting time and just ask for a bar.

"Thirty-five."

He whistled. "That's a lot." *No kidding.* I needed him to tell me how many he wanted, or I'd have to leave and race home.

He said the one thing I never expected. "I'll take them all." He pulled out his wallet and handed me thirty-five dollars!

I didn't know what to say — I couldn't move. Never in a million years did I think someone would buy all my chocolate. I certainly didn't think Mr. Hunter would be the one to buy most of them.

"So now you've got my money…" Mr. Hunter said, rubbing his chin. I knew he was going to ask me to do something for him, like wash his car or lick his boots. I won't lie — I was willing to do it. He had saved me from certain death.

"Are you going to give me my candy?" he asked.

I looked at the two boxes in my hands and

realized in my excitement I forgot to give them to him! I shoved them in front of me. "I'm sorry. Here you go."

He grabbed them and said, "These are mine now, right? I can do what I want with them?"

That was a silly question. Of course he could do whatever he wanted with them. For all I cared, he could throw them in the trash. "Yes, sir. They're yours."

He smiled. "I'd like to welcome you and your mom to the neighborhood with these two boxes of chocolate." He handed them right back to me.

I wasn't sure what to do. I already had his money. Now I had the candy back too? I stared at him, confused.

"Please take them," Mr. Hunter pleaded. "I'll never hear the end of it from my wife if you don't. There's not enough Aspirin in the world for that." He smirked. "Trust me — you're doing me a favor."

"Thank you," was all I could say to him. He wasn't a bad guy. I was liking the neighborhood more and more and wished we didn't have to leave.

SATURDAY NIGHT

My mom wasn't home yet when I got back. I was drenched in sweat and out of breath from running home. It was worth it, though. My mom would be so proud of me.

I heard her car door close in the driveway. She came inside and didn't even see me. "Hey, Jonah," was all she said before she went straight to the computer.

"Mom, what's going on?" I asked her. I looked over her shoulder and saw she was on the bank's website.

"I got an alert on my phone from the bank," she said. "It says the account balance fell below twenty dollars." She sounded frustrated. "I don't know how this happened."

I smiled because I was about to make her day. "I can tell you what happened." I held the two boxes of chocolate in front of her like a trophy.

She stared at me and shook her head. I don't think I've ever seen her look so disappointed. "You used my card to buy candy?" She put her hands on top of her head. "Please tell me this is joke. Because I know you would not use that card unless it was an emergency."

I swallowed hard. She was speaking slowly again, and she never spoke that slowly unless I was in trouble. I had a feeling I was in trouble no matter what I told her. "It's okay. I know you didn't want me selling candy door to door, but that's what I did while you were gone. And I made a lot of money!"

Her face turned red.

I reached into my pockets and pulled out the money I had collected. "Look. I sold it all and even got to keep some." I showed her the money, but she wouldn't stop staring at me.

She said something she had never said before. "I don't know what to do with you. Go to your room until I can figure it out."

I handed her the money, but she wouldn't take it — so I set it on the desk next to the computer. I marched toward my room, with every intention of slamming my door shut and locking myself in. I went out of my way to help, and that was the thanks I got for it? Never again!

"Jonah, wait," I heard my mom plead. I stopped and turned around. What else was she going to yell at me about?

She stared at me and grinned. "I got the job."

I couldn't help but grin back. "I knew you would."

She stood up and shook her head. "I don't want to be mad at you. Things are hard right now." She walked over and hugged me. "Thank you for trying to help out."

As I lay in my lumpy bed that night, I wondered how much more our lives would change. We didn't have a lot at the moment, but at least we had each other.

SUNDAY MORNING

I woke up to a rap on my bedroom window. I smiled when I saw the fox's blue eyes staring back at me, standing outside with his face pressed against the window and his tongue sticking out again.

I sat up and stretched, trying to get the kinks out of my back. The sun was out, so there wasn't any crunching under my feet as I walked to the window. I unlocked the window and pushed it up.

"Good morning, fox," I told him. My voice was shaky because the air outside was cool.

"Wanna have some fun today?" he asked, wagging his tail. His smile was so big I had to laugh. He made me feel good about myself for some reason.

"I don't think I'm allowed to have fun today," I told him, hoping I was wrong. I had never seen my mom as mad as she was the night before. And I didn't know what she had planned for me that day.

"I'm in trouble."

The fox's smile disappeared and his tail stopped wagging. "I hate to hear that." He looked around the side of the house. "Don't forget to unlock the chicken coop. Gotta make sure they're happy and healthy." He licked his lips for some reason.

"I may never see you again," I confided in him.

"Jonah!" my mom yelled from the kitchen. "Come get some breakfast!"

"Wait," the fox said. "What are you talking about?"

I shrugged my shoulders at the fox. "I've gotta go."

I closed the window and waved to him. I was never good at goodbyes. I had left Orlando without telling any of my friends I was leaving. It hurt too much.

The fox looked sad and confused with his ears down and his tail between his legs. Did he not want me to go either?

"Jonah!" my mom yelled again.

"Coming!" I yelled back.

I turned from the window and marched out of my bedroom. I felt weak and tired. I did not want to leave my new friend behind.

"I'm going into work this morning," my mom said when I sat at the kitchen table. She had a plate of pancakes waiting for me. "I won't be back until tonight." That got my attention. I would have time with the fox after all.

"I've asked your uncle Mike to check in on you this afternoon if he can." She stood behind me and put her hands on my shoulders. "The only reason you're not going over there is because I'm making him clean up his place before we move in with him." I could feel her shaking her head. "It's littered with beer cans and cigarettes."

She walked around the table and sat across from me. "I may have overreacted yesterday, and I apologize for that." She nodded her head slowly again. "You know what the rules are, and I'm going to trust you." She stopped nodding. "Please don't make me regret it."

I couldn't help but notice one of my chocolate boxes was empty in the trash can. "What happened to the candy?" I asked, pointing to the box.

"I don't know," she claimed, shrugging her shoulders. "Someone must have eaten them." I knew she loved chocolate, but fifteen bars eaten since last night? That had to be a world record!

"I'm not judging," I said, shoveling the pancakes into my mouth. They were perfect with butter melted over them and maple syrup dripping over the sides.

She smirked and stood back up. "I'm taking the other box of chocolate bars to work with me. I want to make sure they feel loved." She stood next to me and kissed my cheek. "Write your paper and stay out of trouble today." She tightened one of her earrings. "I baked a pan of chicken for the day. Save me a couple of pieces for when I get home tonight."

And then just like that she was gone. I rushed to the bathroom to wash my face and brush my teeth. I didn't want the fox to get a chance to say I smelled like wet farts. They're the worst kind. Usually silent. Always deadly.

I ran out back and passed the outhouse. I didn't see the fox anywhere out there — he'd be back soon. I went ahead and unlocked the chicken coop my mom had locked the night before. Old Nelly looked like she was asleep in the back. I wondered how many rotten eggs she had laid in her lifetime. Hundreds? Thousands?

"Glad you could make it," came the fox's familiar voice from outside the coop.

I stepped out to greet him. "I'm glad I could make it too." I realized I had never asked him the most important question of all. "What's your name?"

The fox rubbed his chin. "I don't know. You're the only person I've ever talked to."

I couldn't help but smile and feel proud. He was the only fox in the world who could talk, and he chose to talk to me. "We should call you *Fox*. Just to keep things from getting confusing"

His blue eyes lit up. "Sounds original." He was trying to hide it, but I could tell he was excited to be named and recognized. It wasn't hard to figure it out. His tail was wagging like a jet fan.

"Did you get enough of what you need?" he asked me.

I wasn't sure what he meant. I kept thinking it was odd none of the chickens came out of the coop.

They were hiding from something.

"You said you didn't have enough money," he reminded me. I remembered our conversation a couple of days earlier. That's when I had decided to sell the candy.

"Not quite," I admitted. Forty dollars wasn't enough to fill up the gas tank in the car. My mom always made me fill it up. She paid for it, of course.

"There's another way you can get more money," Fox said. He stepped up close to me and whispered like he had a secret to share. "If you dig a hole deep enough over there," he said, pointing to the fence line out of view, "you'll reach China. And you know what they have in China?"

Call me crazy, but I was pretty sure Fox was trying to play a practical joke on me. I decided to play his little game. "What?"

"Gold!" he shouted. "Lots of gold!"

I laughed at him so hard my stomach hurt. He wasn't smiling anymore and seemed disappointed I didn't believe him. "Fox, everyone knows you can only find gold at the end of rainbows." *Duh*!

His blue eyes shifted from side to side. "They have lots of rainbows in China." He waved his paws overhead in an arc. "Tons of them. Every day."

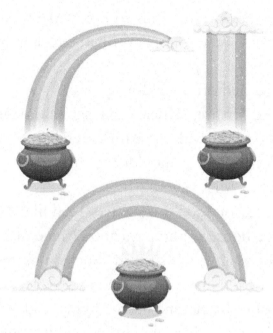

I thought about it for a second and wondered if it could be true. "How long would it take to get there?"

Fox wagged his tail again. "An hour at the most." That wasn't bad. Even if he was pulling my leg, it was only an hour of my life. But I couldn't escape this nagging feeling in the back of head that none of this was true. That it was impossible.

"Jonah!" a man's voice yelled from the house. "Where are you?" I recognized it as my uncle Mike. I heard the back door shut and shoes or boots walking through the leaves toward us. What was he doing there so early? My mom said he wouldn't be there until the afternoon!

"You should run," I urged Fox. "Meet me later." Uncle Mike liked to hunt and I had a feeling foxes were on his list.

Fox dashed off on all four paws.

"There you are," Uncle Mike said moments later, walking up to me with his arms extended. I hugged him, looking over his shoulder to make sure Fox was out of view. "Missed you, pal."

"Missed you too," I admitted. I led him back toward the house so there was no chance of Fox being spotted. I hadn't seen my uncle in more than a year. He looked like he had aged twenty years in that time. Most of his hair had turned gray, and wrinkles covered his face. My mom always said it would happen one day with all the smoking and drinking he did.

"Your mom wanted me to check on you," he said. "Make sure you're okay." He looked over my arms and legs. "I don't see any broken bones."

I shrugged my shoulders. "I'll try harder next time."

He laughed and patted my arm. "We're gonna move you and your mom into my place tomorrow night. That way you don't have to miss any school tomorrow."

Yeah. Thanks a lot.

"Are you gonna to be okay today?" he asked.

"I've got a lot to do, but you can come with me if you're bored."

Not a chance. If this was the last day I could talk with Fox, then I wasn't going anywhere. "I'm fine. I've got your number if I need it."

He patted me on the shoulder. "My man. See you tomorrow night." He went back through the house and left.

I fell flat on my butt when I turned around and Fox was standing right behind me. His paws were raised in an attack position. "You gave me a heart attack!"

He burst out laughing. "Chinese sneak attack!"

It took a minute for me to catch my breath. I realized how hot it was getting as the sun rose higher. "We should go inside and cool down," I tried to persuade Fox.

He looked back at the chicken coop. None of them had come out yet. Maybe they didn't like the heat either. "Okay. But just for a little while. I'll catch some lunch later."

SUNDAY AFTERNOON

"What's that sound?" Fox asked, jumping when the air conditioner turned on and began pumping cold air out of the kitchen vents. He crouched on all fours like he was ready to take off running.

I held out my hands and tried to calm him down. "It's just the air conditioner. It keeps the air cool in here when it's hot outside."

"You can change the air?" he asked in awe. I laughed at the fact he didn't know things like that. "Witchcraft," he muttered as he stood back up on his two hind legs and eyed the room suspiciously.

I was happy to have him back inside. There were so many things to learn about him. And it looked like he had a lot of things he could learn from me. "What do you want to do? My mom's not here."

"The other human is never here," Fox observed. "This is your own den." I could only shrug my shoulders at him. My mom was there when I needed her and that's what counted. "What did you mean when you said you'll never see me again?"

I didn't want to talk about it, but I owed him an explanation. I took a deep breath. "I'm leaving with my mom tomorrow night."

Fox's tail was between his legs again. "You're leaving? Is it because of me?"

"It has nothing to do with you," I tried to convince him. "I begged my mom to stay here, but we don't have enough money." I felt tired and weak again, telling the one creature in the world who I wanted to spend time with that I'd never see him again after that night.

He didn't say anything and sat at the kitchen table. His eyes were a darker shade of blue.

"Anyways," I told him, walking to the refrigerator and trying to avoid this conversation, "I'm going to make a sandwich."

"I'm a wild animal," Fox said in a low voice. "I'm dangerous. I take what I want when I want it. I'll never be cold and I'll never be hungry."

I had no idea how to respond to him. He was hurting as much as I was. "You want a sandwich too?"

"That'd be great," Fox said, his eyes lighting back up. "I'm so hungry I could eat anything. And can you turn the air conditioner off? It's freezing in here!" I smiled when he broke out into laughter.

I sat back down at the kitchen table and slid a

ham sandwich to him. He stared at it like it was an alien. He pulled the top piece of bread off and tossed it to the floor. Then he yanked the slice of ham off and ripped it apart between his teeth before swallowing it. It was the most awesome thing I had ever seen!

"Chicken is better," Fox muttered.

I remembered what my mom had said before she left. "There's a whole pan of chicken in the fridge. You want some?"

Fox sat up straight and stared at the refrigerator like it was the Holy Grail. "You keep chickens in there?"

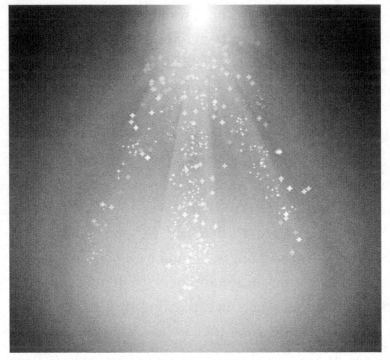

I laughed at his misunderstanding. "Not live chickens. It's just their legs and thighs."

He licked his lips. "You cut them up then store them in that magic box?" He jumped out of his seat and walked toward the fridge. "This is amazing. I've got to get one of these."

"I guess," I said, scratching my head. It wasn't amazing to me, but that's because I had always had one. Fox, on the other hand, looked like he was going to pass out.

"Let me see," he pleaded, standing in front of the fridge. "I have to see it."

I didn't know what the big deal was, so I went ahead and opened it in front of him. His faced changed from excitement to confusion.

"Where are the chickens?" he asked, looking through every shelf desperately. "You said there were chickens."

I shook my head. "I said there were chicken legs and thighs." I pointed to the foil covered pan on the bottom shelf. It had ten chicken pieces on it.

"That's not chicken," Fox complained. "Where are the feathers? You tricked me because I tried to trick you about the gold in China." He huffed and stepped back. "Well played, Joe. Well played."

I tried my best not to laugh at him. "All the feathers are pulled out first, and then it's cooked."

He slammed the refrigerator door shut and stomped into the living room. "More witchcraft!"

I couldn't stop smiling when I joined him in the living room. There were so many things I could teach him. He had learned a lot of things in life — he even learned how to talk! But there were so many things people did and had in their lives every day that he'd never seen. Why did we have to leave tomorrow? I needed more time.

"What's this thing?" Fox asked, banging his paws against the TV remote control.

I snatched it from him before he broke it. I pointed the remote at our fifty-two inch TV and pressed the power button.

I swear to you, Fox's head touched the ceiling when the TV blasted on at full volume, and he jumped sky high. I turned it down right away. He scurried behind the couch and poked his head out every few seconds to look at the cartoons playing on the TV.

"It's okay," I assured him. "It's not real." I couldn't think of a way to explain it to him without him just watching it. I sat on the couch and waited for him to come out.

It took another hour before he walked around the couch and joined me on it. "I wasn't scared," he said, shaking his head. "No, sir."

Right. It took him a while to warm up to the cartoons, but a few hours later he was laughing at them with me. At one point I glanced at the table in front of us and saw the paper I started writing last night.

"I need to write something for school," I explained to Fox, leaning toward the table so I could write the three paragraphs. "It might take me a while. Are you okay?"

He stared at the cartoons and brushed a paw at me. "Yeah, yeah. Do whatever you have to do." He laughed at the TV. "They're so silly."

I'd only known Fox for a couple of days and I just showed him some modern technology that day. Was I a bad person because I already had him addicted to TV?

I'd have to worry about that later. He was having a good time, and I was hanging out with him. Now if I only knew what to write about my best friend.

I had no idea, so I came to the only logical conclusion. I had to write about Tommy. He was my best friend in the second grade. I was new at my school and no one knew my past. Tommy was the perfect answer.

I wrote three paragraphs about him in less than an hour. It only took that long because I went back and double checked the spelling and grammar. That left one question in my mind because I had plenty of time left. *Do I really want to write Shane's paper?*

Fox tapped me on the shoulder. "Where did the cartoons go?" The TV screen had a message flashing on it.

WE'VE EXPERIENCED A TEMPORARY INTERRUPTION OF YOUR SERVICES.

I'd only seen that message once before, and that's when my mom forgot to pay the cable bill. I had an idea what was going on this time. "My mom had it turned off since we're leaving tomorrow. Sorry."

He huffed and looked at my paper. "Did you finish?"

I did, but I still had the other decision to make. I had butterflies in my stomach just thinking about it. "I think so. I'm not sure."

"You know what I do when I'm not sure about something?" he asked.

I had no idea. "What?"

"I go ahead and do it," he said, smiling. "There's no rule that says I can't change my mind later."

He was a fox, but his advice made complete sense. I went ahead and wrote Shane's paper for him right then and there in record time. They were the best three paragraphs I'd ever written — what a shame to waste them on someone else! I didn't know if it was the right decision, but I could always change my mind before class started the next day.

"Thanks, Fox," I told him.

My mom's car squeaked when it stopped in the driveway. *Oh no!* Was it already time for her to come home? That day had flown by so fast. I did not want it to end.

"You have to go, Fox," I urged him, pointing behind me. "Out the back door."

He jumped off the couch and landed on all four paws. What he said next left me speechless. "If you ever need a friend — just look for me." He dashed out of the living room and through the kitchen before I could say anything. I knew he was already out the back door and where he was supposed to be. I couldn't believe he was gone and I'd never see him again.

SUNDAY NIGHT

"I'm so glad to be home," my mom said, taking her shoes off and lying on the couch. She looked exhausted. "I had the longest day."

I half smiled. "I'm glad you're home too." I loved my mom, and I was always happy to see her, but I wished she had stayed at work a little longer.

"I see you finished your paper," she said, waving a hand at the table.

I looked at the table and freaked out. There was only one sheet of paper on the table. I had written two! One for me and one for Shane! Where was the second one?

"Can I read it?" my mom asked.

I picked up the paper and lost my breath. It was the one I had written for Shane! I wiped away a bead of sweat from my forehead. "I'm still working on it."

She stood up and stretched. "Let me know when you're done. I'm going to eat some of the chicken in the fridge and head to bed." She winked at me and walked toward the kitchen. "Big day for everyone tomorrow."

I waited until she was out of the living room, then sprang into action. My paper had to be around there somewhere. I searched the entire living room floor and looked beneath the couch. It was nowhere!

I felt sick when I sat on the couch and remembered

what Fox had said. *I'm so hungry I could eat anything.* Did he snatch it before he ran off? Why was this happening to me? It was Sunday night, and I was out of time to write anything else. My night couldn't get any worse.

"Jonah Johnson!" my mom yelled from the kitchen. "Get in here right now!"

What was she yelling about? I hadn't done anything wrong. I gulped because she only used my full name when I was in big trouble. I took a deep breath and went into the kitchen.

My night *did* get worse!

The refrigerator door was wide open and the chicken pan was on the floor. It was empty — the ten thighs and legs were gone!

"Please explain this to me," my mom said in a low voice. "I could swear I asked you to save some chicken for me tonight." She shook her head and stared at me with wide eyes. "What's going on with you? First you disobeyed me with the candy. And now this?"

I stared back at her as I tried to think of an explanation. Fox had decided to eat the chicken after all. Did he gobble it all down in record time before he ran out of the house?

"You've written your paper and you've had plenty to eat," she said, pointing to the empty pan. "Go to your room and think about what you've done. I don't know what to do with you."

That's when I came to the only decision that could save me. I told her the truth. "It was the fox." I told her the entire story from when I met Fox up until that moment.

She put a hand on her forehead. "Now you're telling lies?" she asked with a broken voice. She couldn't stop blinking. Was she crying? "Go, Jonah. Just go. Go to your room."

I tried to plead with her to believe me, but she waved me off. I marched out of the kitchen, through the living room, and straight to my bedroom. I slammed the door shut and jumped on my lumpy bed.

It was a good thing we were leaving the next day. Fox was my friend and he was awesome, but I'd never been in as much trouble as I was since I met him.

I grunted when I realized I had left Shane's paper on the living room table. I did not want my mom to see it because she was already in a bad mood. I got out of bed, cracked my door open, and listened to make sure she wasn't around.

It was safe. I'd grab the paper and rush back.

I could hear my mom talking on her phone in the kitchen, so I grabbed the paper off the table and tiptoed my way back. Before I got out of the living room, I overheard her.

"I don't know what to do with him," she said to the other person. "I didn't raise him to be a liar. Maybe I made a mistake moving him from the city to the country. I want him to be happy."

My heart broke because I wanted my mom to be happy too. I went back to my room and stared out the window. For all the trouble Fox had caused me, I still wanted to see him again. He made me happy. My mom didn't make a mistake bringing me there. I never wanted to leave.

MONDAY MORNING

I clutched my backpack as I walked through the school halls. It still felt odd to me, as I'd only been there once before. I was surrounded by kids I didn't know and none of them acknowledged me. I felt invisible.

"Hey, Jonah!" someone shouted from behind me. I didn't have to turn around to know it was Shane. I didn't bother to correct him about my name that time.

He stepped in front of me and put a hand on my chest to stop me. Sam was by his side. "Not so fast. Where's my paper?"

I had tossed and turned all night in my lumpy bed, trying to decide if I should give the paper to him. I didn't want to get beat up, and I didn't want him to take advantage of me for the rest of the year. I couldn't get Melissa's voice out of my head from the farmers market: *Do yourself a favor and stay away from Shane. He doesn't do any of his own work. Someone has to stand up to him.*

I pulled my backpack around and held it in front of me. I looked at the big kid and thought about it for a second. Fox had told me that I could change my mind if I wanted to. I decided to go with the decision I had made the night before.

I unzipped my backpack, pulled the paper out, and handed it to Shane without saying anything. His face lit up when he grabbed it, and he pushed me back.

"That's what I thought, Jonah." He laughed and looked over at his best friend, Sam. "Sam has something he'd like to ask you."

Sam looked like a soldier with his sailor's haircut. "I've got a science project due in Mr. Wheeler's class next week." He cocked his head and smirked. "I'm gonna need you to do it."

I didn't bother to answer him because I had no intention of doing it. Besides, I was never any good at science.

The class bell rang and all the kids scattered into their classrooms. Shane pulled Sam back toward Miss Cox's class. "What a loser," he said.

I followed them into the class and took the same seat in the front I had on Friday. Melissa was next to me again and smiling with her big dimples.

"Hi, Joe," she said. "It's good to see you again." I believed her, so I smiled back. I didn't want to tell her I had written Shane's paper for him, but she'd figure it out.

"Good morning, class," Miss Cox said to all of us. She was sitting behind her desk and smiling. It was going to take some time to get used to her high-pitched country twang. "Did everyone finish their papers?"

I was embarrassed to admit I didn't have a paper, so I didn't say anything. I was hoping it would take the entire class time for others to read their papers and Miss Cox wouldn't get to me. It would give me time to write my paper that night and bring it in the next day. Was that too much to hope for?

"Who wants to go first? Any volunteers?" Miss Cox asked, scanning the room. Everyone fell silent. "Anyone?"

Melissa raised her hand. She was brave. "I'll do it."

"Thank you, Melissa," Miss Cox said. "The class is yours."

Melissa stood up and walked in front of the chalkboard then turned around to face the class. She cleared her throat and smiled at me. For the first time I realized how cute she was.

"My best friend is my cousin, Millie," she read aloud from her paper. "We grew up together and like the same things. She goes to a different school, but we see each other all the time."

I don't have any cousins. My uncle Mike never got married. He always said girls were the devil. Except for my mom, who was his sister — she was an angel.

"That's why Millie will always be my best friend," Melissa finished. The class clapped for her. Had I missed most of what she said? I hated getting lost in my thoughts and losing track of time. My mom had the same problem and said it was a sign of being a genius.

"Thank you, Melissa," Miss Cox said when Melissa handed the paper to her. "That was very well done." She looked at the paper for a minute then set it down on her desk. "Who's next?" she asked the class.

The room was silent again.

"No volunteers?" she asked like she was surprised. I was only eleven years old, but I knew no one volunteered to do something they didn't want to do. What was so shocking about that?

"Shane," she said. "Come on up."

I didn't turn around to face him because I didn't want to see the stupid smirk on his face. It was too late to change my mind, and it made me feel sick. My heart was racing.

"You're the next lucky contestant," I heard Sam laughing as Shane passed by.

Shane stood in front of the chalkboard and winked at me. I wasn't sure if that meant he was grateful or if he was trying to show he was better than me. It's not fair if you think about it. He didn't do any of the work and was about to get all of the credit for that paper.

"You're gonna love this," Shane said to Miss Cox. "I put a lot of work into it."

"Go ahead, Shane," Miss Cox said. "We don't have a lot of time." I was glad to hear that. He could take as much time as he wanted.

He held the paper in front of him dramatically. "My best friend. By Shane Connors." He looked around the paper and winked at me again.

And then he read exactly what I wrote for him.

"My best friend is my mommy. She dresses me every morning and changes my wet sheets."

The class burst out in laughter.

As I was tossing and turning in my lumpy bed the night before, I realized I could never let someone else take advantage of me. I had to give him the paper.

Shane stared at me like he was trying to burn a hole through my head. The class was still laughing at him, and Miss Cox was trying to make them stop. "I didn't write this," Shane said while he was staring at me with hatred.

Miss Cox looked back and forth from him to me like she was trying to figure out why Shane wouldn't take his eyes off of me. She focused on me and shook her head like she knew exactly what was going on.

"Shane," she said to him, "are you saying someone else wrote your paper?"

He smiled because he must have realized Miss Cox figured everything out. "That's right."

Miss Cox cleared her throat and stood up. "Someone's in big trouble."

I gulped. I was already in so much trouble with my mom. Once she found out about this — my life was over.

"Shane," Miss Cox continued, "you're already behind in this class. If you're telling me that you didn't write that paper, then I'm gonna have to fail you." I think she winked at me from the corner of her eye.

Shane lowered the paper. His mouth was wide open.

"I'm going to ask you one more time," she said. "Did you write that paper?"

Shane rubbed his forehead like he couldn't think of the right answer. After a minute, he stopped and stared at the floor. "Yes. I wrote it."

"Keep reading!" his friend Sam shouted. "We want to hear the whole thing!"

The class cheered and broke out into laughter again. Shane stood there, hanging his head.

Miss Cox held up a hand for the room to be silent. She looked like she wanted to laugh, but did everything she could to keep from doing it. "Shane doesn't look like he feels very good. I'll go ahead and take that paper."

He looked grateful when he handed it to her then headed back toward the class. He made sure to stop by my desk. "You're dead meat," he whispered.

I ignored him and stared at the chalkboard like I didn't know what he was talking about. I was scared out of my mind because I had no doubt he had every intention of beating me up after school. Now I just wanted to go home.

"Joe," Miss Cox said. "Let's hear your paper. I'm sure it's very entertaining."

I couldn't move. She didn't know I didn't have a paper and I didn't want to admit it. She knew I was a writer and had faith I could do it over the weekend. I swallowed hard. "I don't have it." I whispered my only excuse. "My fox ate my homework."

A couple of kids snickered. "I hate it when that happens," one kid complained.

"I see," Miss Cox said. "Do you remember what you wrote?"

The truth was I did. It was about my friendship with Tommy in the second grade. I wrote it in minutes because it flowed out my mind with ease. "Every word."

She motioned toward the chalkboard. "Come up here and tell us about it. I can at least give you some of the credit."

I was leery to do it, but if it kept me out of trouble then I didn't have any other choice. All I had to do was get out of my seat, walk up to the chalkboard, and tell everyone about my old best friend Tommy.

There was just one problem. I was scared out of my mind to speak in front of a bunch of people I didn't know yet. I had once heard it was easier to speak in front of a crowd if you imagined everyone naked. I doubted it was true because I didn't want to imagine *anyone* naked!

"What's it going to be?" Miss Cox asked.

Melissa leaned across her desk and touched my arm. "You can do it, Joe. I believe in you." The way she said it made me believe in myself.

I stood up, took a deep breath, and walked to the chalkboard. When I turned around, all I could see were hundreds of eyes looking back at me. There were less than thirty kids there, but it felt like a lot more! The room seemed so small at that moment.

"Go ahead, Joe," Miss Cox said. "We're almost out of time." That was just great. I was going to be the last one making a speech that day. If only one other person could have gone before me!

"My best friend's name is…" I froze when I remembered what Fox said to me the night before. *If you ever need a friend — just look for me.*

I started over again with words I never wrote. "My best friend's name is Fox. I've only known him for a few days, but I feel like I've known him my entire life. He's taught me a lot of things about myself, and there are many more things I want to show him."

I looked through the class with more confidence. "Fox has taught me to laugh at myself and not take life too seriously. He's taught me to go after the things I want in life and achieve what I never thought was possible." I smiled when I thought of one other thing. "He's taught me to stay away from rotten eggs because they smell like wet farts."

Everyone in class laughed! Even Miss Cox couldn't keep a straight face. I did my best to keep talking without laughing with them.

"I don't know if I'll ever see Fox again, but he'll always be my best friend." I remembered how Mrs. Hunter got her husband to buy the chocolate from me. My great-grandma had been her best friend, and even though my great-grandma wasn't around anymore, Mrs. Hunter would always do what she could to help her family. That was true friendship.

"He feels like family to me now," I said to the class. "Maybe that's what a best friend really is."

Miss Cox stood up and smiled. "That was very nice, Joe. Thank you." Some of the kids clapped for me.

I went back to my desk and sat down. Melissa told me that I did an amazing job. I didn't know if it was amazing or not, but I meant everything I had said. I didn't want that day to end. Because when it did, I knew I'd never see my best friend again.

MONDAY AFTERNOON

My uncle Mike picked me up from school that afternoon. I was glad I didn't have to take a long trip home with my mom while she was mad at me. I should have never told her about Fox. I don't know why I expected her to believe such a crazy story.

My stomach churned as we got closer to the house. We were going to pack up our belongings and leave forever.

"How was school?" my uncle asked.

It turned out to be a pretty good day. I didn't get into trouble for not having my paper. I became better friends with Melissa. Shane went home early because he told the school nurse he had never felt so sick in his life. I knew the real reason he left was because he was too embarrassed to stay at school.

"It was okay."

When we got home, I walked as slow as I could inside. I felt drained.

"There you are," my mom said when we walked in. Mr. and Mrs. Hunter were sitting on the couch with her. They both said 'hi' to me.

My uncle Mike put a hand on my shoulder. "I'll load some of these boxes in the truck." He pointed to the boxes along the wall that he and my mom must have packed. There weren't many because this house had already been furnished the way my great-grandma had left it. We mostly had clothes and kitchen utensils packed up.

"Use the restroom if you need to," my mom said to me. "We're leaving in about an hour."

I put my backpack down. I hadn't eaten anything all day with the butterflies in my stomach. I didn't have an appetite. "I'm good."

"We hate to see you leave, dear," Mrs. Hunter said to my mom. "I wish you had more time."

So did I.

Mr. Hunter's knees cracked when he stood up and came over to me. "Maybe it's for the best," he said to everyone. "This house is older than I am." He grinned and chuckled. "It even survived the Great Depression of the thirties."

I remembered learning about the Great

Depression at my last school in the city. The stock market had crashed, and a lot of people lost their money. It affected everyone and made life really hard.

Mr. Hunter stood in front of me. "We came by because we were going to ask you if you could watch our place for us while we're gone. Mow the lawn. Water the plants." He shook his head. "We're going up to our home in Wyoming for the spring and summer. Oh well."

Now I knew for sure life wasn't fair. They would have paid me to do it!

"Let's go," he said to his wife. She said her goodbyes and joined him by the door. He knocked twice on the wooden doorframe. "Yep. Older than dirt."

"Thank you for the money," I told him as they walked out. I was referring to the thirty-five dollars he gave me for the chocolate.

He winked at me and looked over the house from the outside. "She really is old. Back when she was built, people didn't have a lot of money and didn't trust the banks." He shook his head and pulled his wife along. "A lot of them kept their money under their mattresses."

I froze.

My lumpy mattress.

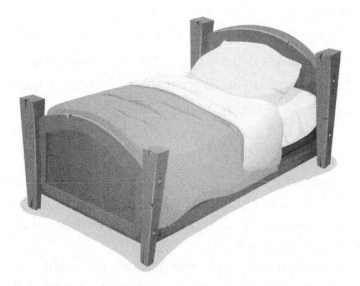

I rushed inside and told my mom to meet me in my bedroom. I was breathing hard, and she asked me if I was okay. I didn't know yet.

Was it possible? My great-grandma had died without a penny to her name. She didn't have any bank accounts, but she survived for decades selling rotten eggs. Did she have money hidden all along?

I stared at my lumpy mattress when my mom walked into my room. "Is everything okay?" she asked. "We need to finish packing and get on the road."

My heart wouldn't stop racing. I felt like I was going to faint. "I need your help. We need to push this mattress up against the wall."

She made a tsking sound with her tongue. "We're not taking that with us. Uncle Mike has a bed for you."

I looked up at her and pleaded with my eyes. "I know you don't believe everything I've told you lately. But I need you to trust me right now. I have to see what's beneath this mattress."

She looked at me and nodded her head. "Okay, Jonah."

We stood side by side and pushed with all of our strength to heave the mattress up against the wall. I almost lost my balance and collapsed beneath the monstrous weight.

We stood back and stared at what was left beneath the mattress. I looked up at my mom and smiled. Her eyes looked they were about to explode out of her head.

More money than I had ever seen lay in front of us. It was dollar bills stacked in ones, fives, twenties, fifties, and hundreds! There were more stacks than I could count.

"Mom," I said, gasping for air. "Is this enough of what we need?"

She smiled and wrapped her arms around me. She screamed like she was at a rock and roll concert. That was awesome!

"It's more than enough," she said in a broken voice. "We don't have to leave!" She let go of me and danced around the room, laughing in a way I'd never heard. She was the happiest I'd ever seen her.

I reached down and touched a stack of cash to make sure it was real. This kind of thing didn't happen to kids like me. I had never even won a game of duck, duck, goose.

It felt like gold in my fingers. I couldn't wait to tell Fox that I didn't have to dig a hole to China. We could be best friends forever now.

MONDAY NIGHT

My mom cooked my favorite dinner that night — fried chicken, mashed potatoes, and buttery biscuits. She danced around the kitchen and hummed a happy tune I'd never heard. She banged the pot lids together like they were cymbals.

I stood there and smiled while I watched her, knowing she could keep living her childhood dream. She thought she had lost this house and its memories forever, but now it would always be hers. Nothing could take away her happiness.

Someone tapped on the front door.

"See who that is!" my mom shouted, dancing to her own beat. "Maybe they heard me singing and want my autograph!" She threw her head up, laughed like a crazy person, and whipped the mashed potatoes.

I shook my head. I didn't have the heart to tell her that her singing was worse than mine when I was in the shower.

I opened the front door and froze.

Fox stood on the other side on all four paws. That reminded me of the first time I had seen him. He was magnificent with his bright brown hair and aqua blue eyes and wide smile. I nearly collapsed like I had that first night.

"You shouldn't be here," I whispered to him. I turned to see if my mom had noticed him. She wasn't any wiser — she was doing the salsa dance like a zombie.

"I smell chicken," Fox said. "I'm starving."

I crossed my arms and shook my head at him. He knew better than to come there when my mom was around. It was for his own protection. "I'll bring you some later. Wait for me out back."

"Did it come from the magic box?" he asked.

I knew he was talking about the refrigerator. I hung my head. "Yes." I started to close the door.

He licked his lips then slid through the doorway right past me. What was he doing? I had no idea how my mom would react when she saw him.

I ran into the kitchen and waved my hands in front of her to get her attention. She stopped dancing but swayed her shoulders from side to side. "Loosen up," she whined.

95

"Don't be a party pooper." She started to dance again, but stopped when she looked over the kitchen counter.

Fox was staring at her with his bright blue eyes. She grabbed my chest and held me back. "Don't move," she whispered. "It could be dangerous." She was breathing hard.

"What are you talking about?" I asked her. "This is Fox. I told you about him the other night."

She pushed me behind her toward the back door. "That fox is not your friend. It's a wild animal and could have rabies." She reached into her pants pocket and pulled out her cell phone.

"Hello?' she said into the receiver. "Mike? Get here as fast as you can with your gun."

This was not going well. I had to find a way to make her believe everything I told her about Fox. I couldn't lose my best friend. I snatched the cell phone from my mom and threw it across the room.

"Jonah!" she shouted. "Why did you do that?" She took a deep breath. "It's okay. You've been under a lot of stress."

"He's my best friend, Mom," I told her. "You can't hurt him."

She opened the door and motioned for me to slip out. "He's a wild animal, Jonah. He's not a pet. He's not a dog." She was doing her best to convince me as she pushed me out the door. "If he was then he'd have a collar. Where's his collar?"

My uncle Mike would be there any minute, and he wouldn't hesitate to shoot Fox. I had to stop this before it was too late. "Tell her!" I shouted at Fox. "Tell her the truth!"

Fox stared at me for a moment then looked around like he wanted to make sure no one else was watching. He stood up slowly on his two hind legs and looked squarely at my mom.

"I don't know," he said. "Where's *your* collar?"

My mom shrieked and put a hand on the wall beside us for balance. I was glad because I wasn't sure if I was strong enough to catch her if she fell. Her mouth was wide upon, and her chest heaved up and down.

"It's okay, Mom," I assured her, nodding my head
slowly — the same way she did at me when she wanted to
make sure I understood something . She tried to grab me as
I walked around her and over to Fox. I stood by Fox's side
and faced her. "I need you to trust me."

She put a hand on her chest and waited for her
breathing to slow down. Her legs were wobbly, like she
couldn't stand much longer. She cleared her throat and
looked back and forth from me to Fox.

"What do you want with us?" she asked Fox in a quiet
voice.

He pointed at the kitchen. "Chicken from your magic box."

She looked confused before she stared back at me. "Jonah?" I had no idea what she was going to ask me. The only thing I knew for sure was that we were running out of time. Uncle Mike would be there soon with his gun.

"Yes, Ma'am?" I gulped.

My mom took a deep breath. "Go get another plate for your friend."

I smiled at her and laughed. She smiled back.

"Are we gonna stand around and talk?" Fox asked with his two front paws up in the air. "Or are we gonna eat some chicken?"

My mom shook her head and laughed. She walked over to me and Fox. "I trust you, Jonah. I've always trusted you." She hugged me and bent down to face Fox.

"You're a cute little guy, aren't you?" She stroked his head and rubbed his ears.

"Right there," he said. "Yep. Yep. A little to the left." I laughed at the huge smile on his face while his tail whipped back and forth.

Then my mom said the one thing that let me know everything was okay.

"Any friend of Jonah's is a friend of mine. Welcome to our home."

It's been a few months since I've seen Fox, but now he's back and we're about to get into more trouble than ever before. I just had my twelfth birthday party, and the school bully, Shane, was there. He caught Fox talking to me! Now Fox is in danger, and I'm the only one who can save him.

My Fox Ate My Cake is a funny fantasy with a new adventure that's entertaining for kids of all ages, and adults who secretly never grew up.

AVAILABLE AT AMAZON.COM
Print and Ebook

DAVID BLAZE

You can keep up with everything I'm doing at:

www.davidblazebooks.com

And you can follow me on Facebook. Just search for David Blaze, Children's Author. Be sure to like the page!

If you enjoyed my story, please tell your friends and family. I'd also appreciate it if you'd leave a review on Amazon.com and tell me what you think about my best friend, Fox.

See you soon!

CPSIA information can be obtained
at www.ICGtesting.com
Printed in the USA
FSOW03n2058230617
35610FS